GO BOTS

MIGHTY ROBOTS
MIGHTY VEHICLES

THE POWER MACHINE

Written by Dwight Jon Zimmerman
Illustrated by Leopoldo Durañona

A GOLDEN BOOK • NEW YORK
Western Publishing Company, Inc., Racine, Wisconsin 53404

The trademark GOBOTS and all related character marks and designs are owned by and used under a license agreement with Tonka Corporation. ©Tonka Corporation 1985. All Rights Reserved. Printed in the U.S.A. No part of this book may be reproduced or copied in any form without written permission from the publisher. GOLDEN®, GOLDEN & DESIGN®, A GOLDEN BOOK®, and GOLDEN HEROIC CHAMPIONS™ are trademarks of Western Publishing Company, Inc. Library of Congress Catalog Card Number: 85-80567. ISBN 0-307-16051-3

A B C D E F G H I J

Deep in the hideout of the Renegade GoBots, Professor Braxis, their human ally, was explaining his latest scheme.

"Look at the model of the Saltsea Fresh Water Plant," he said. "It has machinery that can remove the salt from sea water and make it drinkable."

"Bah!" Crasher sneered. "Renegades don't drink water."

"Of course not," said Braxis. "But with the salt you get EnergeX."

"The super-powerful energy compound!" Cy-Kill exclaimed. "We can use it to defeat the Guardians and conquer Earth! How can we get it?"

"With my new invention, the EnergeX Filter!" Professor Braxis said. "You capture the plant, I hook up my machine, and in minutes we start producing all the power we need."

"Perfect!" Cy-Kill said with an evil grin. "Professor Braxis, Cop-Tur will fly you and your invention to the plant. Crasher and I will follow disguised as vehicles."

Meanwhile, at the AstroCorps Motor Pool, Captain Matt Hunter and cadet A.J. Foster were giving lube jobs to Guardian GoBots Leader-1 and Turbo.

"Thank you, Matt," said Leader-1.

"Hush, Leader-1!" A.J. said. "We don't have talking airplanes on Earth! If the authorities find out who you really are, you'll be in big trouble!"

"Nick, what's wrong? You look bored," Scooter said.

"I am," cadet Nick Burns sighed. "There's nothing to do here."

"I have seen very little of Earth, Nick," Scooter said. "Let's go sightseeing. You can tell me all about your planet."

"That's a great idea, Scooter!" Nick shouted happily. And in minutes they were driving down the highway.

Nick and Scooter drove for a while and then stopped to take a break.

"Earth is beautiful," Scooter said. "But I do miss GoBotron. It is a wonderful world filled with many amazing machines, which Cy-Kill and his Renegades tried to wreck."

Scooter added, "Now that we've pursued them to Earth, they seem to be working even harder to wreck things here. I wish we could get rid of them without fighting."

"I do, too," said Nick. "But if there has to be a fight to stop them, we're the ones to do it."

Certain that she had totally wrecked Scooter, Crasher drove back to the Saltsea Fresh Water Plant.

"Scooter, are you all right?" Nick asked.

"Yes, but I can't switch from vehicle to robot," Scooter said.

"I must tell Leader-1 what happened!" Scooter said. But when he tried to use his radio, he discovered that it, too, was damaged. "I don't know if Leader-1 heard me!" he said.

"Let's not wait!" Nick said. "We must discover where the Renegades are — and what they're up to!"

Meanwhile, Professor Braxis and Cop-Tur had reached the Saltsea Fresh Water Plant.

"Once I hook up all these sleeping-gas cans to the central air conditioning unit, no one inside will be able to stay awake!" Professor Braxis said. "Then you can dispose of them, Cop-Tur!"

CENTRAL AIR CONDITIONER

Sleeping Gas

Sleeping Gas

Sleeping Gas

Minutes later, Cy-Kill and Crasher walked in. "Everything is going according to plan," Cy-Kill said. "Hook up your machine, Professor Braxis — now!"

"I will when I'm good and ready, Cy-Kill, and not one second before!" Professor Braxis said, angry at Cy-Kill's bullying.

"And when will that be?" Cy-Kill thundered.

"Right now," Professor Braxis said with a gulp.

"We must stop them," Nick said. "I have a plan. Let's hope your hologram ray still works, Scooter!"

Suddenly, the Renegades heard a noise in the hall.

"Professor Braxis's sleeping gas missed a human!" Crasher shouted. "He's escaping on a scooter!"

"He must not get away!" Cy-Kill shouted. "Stop him!"

"Wait, you fools!" Professor Braxis shouted. "It's a trick! That 'human' is a cave man! Cave men do not exist anymore!"

"Oh, no!" Scooter said to himself. "I made a mistake in my program! I hope Nick has had enough time to reprogram Braxis's machine!"

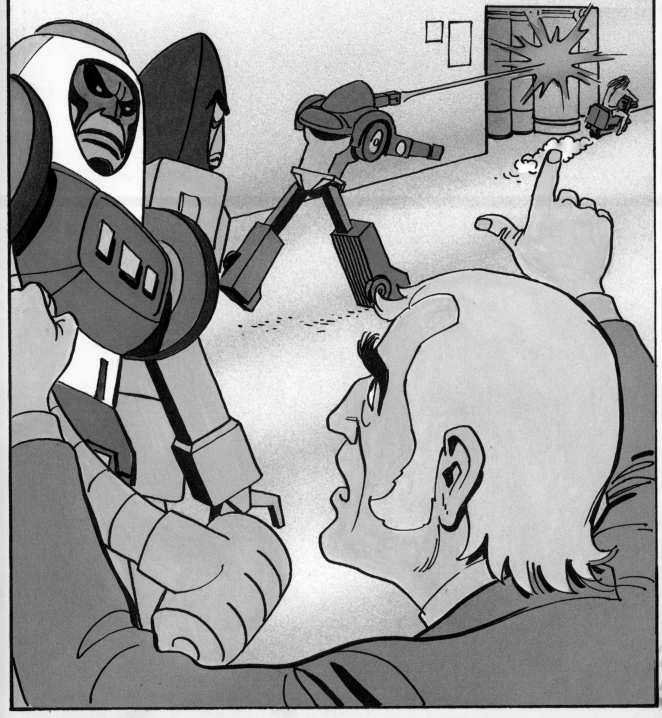

"Professor Braxis made a tough security code, but nothing can stop a super hacker like me!" Nick said. "Now to push this button and . . ."

"Your trick didn't work, Nick Burns!" Professor Braxis said. "Get him, Cop-Tur!"

Nick ran out of the plant and into a nearby orchard. "Cop-Tur will never find me here!" he thought.

But as he watched helplessly, Cop-Tur used his helicopter blades to cut away all the trees.

"You can't escape me!" Cop-Tur boomed.

Meanwhile, inside the plant, Crasher had quickly caught Scooter!

"So, Scooter, it is you who tried to trick us!" Crasher said. "After I get the EnergeX, I'll smash you into a thousand pieces!"

But Scooter was not thinking about his fate. He was worried about the world. "If Leader-1 and Turbo don't show up soon, Earth is doomed!" he thought.

"Let me go, you big hunk of junk!" Nick shouted as Cop-Tur and Crasher brought their prisoners to Cy-Kill.

"Not until we have the EnergeX, human!" Cy-Kill said. Then he angrily turned to Professor Braxis and said, "We have delayed too long! Start the machine!"

"But I must make sure that pesky kid didn't tamper with my program!" Professor Braxis cried.

"Start it!" Cy-Kill shouted angrily.

There was a moment's silence as the machine filled with salt. Then the EnergeX Filter started making loud chugging noises.

"Look — the bag is beginning to fill with EnergeX!" Professor Braxis shouted.

"Now Earth and GoBotron will be crushed beneath the unstoppable power of the Renegades!" Cy-Kill thundered.

"Wrong, Cy-Kill!" said a commanding voice as the plant's outside wall was smashed open.

"It's Leader-1, Turbo, Matt, and A.J.!" Nick shouted. "Yay! They got Scooter's message!"

"Bah!" Crasher shouted. "We will still win! Our fun has just begun!"

"Crasher, I'm going to throw you for a loss!" Turbo said.

But as Crasher fell against the control panel, neither noticed that her elbow had tripped the alarm switch connected to police headquarters!

POLICE ALARM

"You are too late, Leader-1!" Cy-Kill shouted. "I have the EnergeX! Soon I'll be all-powerful!"

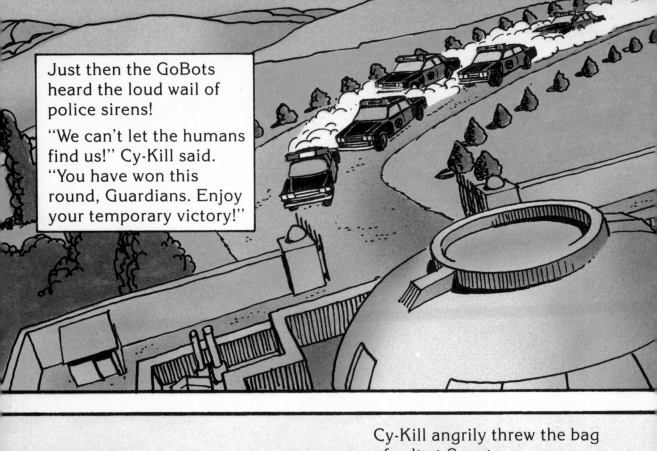

Just then the GoBots heard the loud wail of police sirens!

"We can't let the humans find us!" Cy-Kill said. "You have won this round, Guardians. Enjoy your temporary victory!"

Cy-Kill angrily threw the bag of salt at Scooter.

"I must stop the bag from hitting Scooter!" Matt thought as he jumped to block the bag.

Oof!

"After them, Guardians! We mustn't let them escape!" Leader-1 said.

"Don't worry, Leader-1. We'll catch them before you know it!" Turbo said as he changed into a race car. "Nothing can outrun me on the road!"

No sooner had all the GoBots left than the police began to rush in.

"I hope I can come up with a good story to explain all this," Matt gulped.

"Yes," said Nick. "It looks like we've been left holding the bag — of salt!"